CW00496273

J U J U

Stories By

JUDY MOFFETT

ELIXIR PRESS
P.O. Box 18010
Minneapolis, MN 55418

ACKNOWLEDGMENTS

The following stories originally appeared in the publications below:

"Bad Habits" was published in *The Suisun Valley Review*, vol 18, # 1, spring 1998.

"The Acromegaly Man" appeared in *Lynx Eye* Vol. III, #3, summer 2001.

"Placebo's Good Medicine" was published online in *Small Spiral Notebook,* winter 2003.

"Sins of Omission" appeared in *The Rockhurst Review,* sixteenth edition, spring 2003.

ISBN: 1-932418-01-6

CONTENTS

JUJU

Placebo's Good Medicine

My father believed that he and I were lovers in a past life. Until I turned fourteen, he'd been my best buddy, always showing me some handy trick like how to edit a home movie, identify a bird, or repair a ukulele. One day he stopped talking to me completely, shutting doors behind him wherever he went.

I felt like an overgrown changeling. Twenty-three years later I read his notebooks and it all made sense, if I may apply this term to matters that defy logic.

My mother could cure herself of anything. She never went to doctors, not even when she cracked her kneecap. At the sight of a white lab coat, her blood pressure soared to dangerous levels. If she'd been the one with cancer, I'm quite sure she'd have found a way to talk herself out of it.

Naturally everyone has a good laugh when I say this. Meanwhile patients in clinical trials recover beautifully on sugar pills and medics contemplate pouring them into amber vials with prescription labels and presenting them at the pharmacy counter so the mind can get the wrong idea and set the body right. For the right price of course.

My father had no direct mind-body pipeline. He lacked my mother's instincts for what to eat or avoid, whether to exercise or rest, what tinctures to swallow at bedtime. My mother was well-tended, bouncy, with ringlets of chestnut hair. You couldn't hope for a healthier specimen of a mom. My father who had never been sick a day had grown up with western medicine but his years with my mother rubbed off. When his astonishing diagnosis came down, the MD said "chemo" and "surgery"; my father said "no" and "no."

"No" meant investing hope in measures any doctor would scoff at. My mother excelled at that. She anticipated no problem. They were in this together.

But my father was alone in his body. After all this time it didn't recognize him. "Who are you?" it demanded, "and why should I care?" An interpreter was badly needed. He spoke reason: "e=mc2"; it spoke the dreamy gibberish of the subconscious: "oceanowlfignewtonplankton."

He was a man of double-shelved bookcases, determined to make the most of a lifetime, studying Pueblo Indian cave art, mastering Argentine tango *and* the latest spreadsheet program. He wrote books, taught at universities, spent weeks on the phone fortifying rescue efforts in bedeviled Central American villages. He had opuses in mind, videos in production, murals ready to paint on the walls of government buildings. His agenda was such that he was always ahead of himself, onto the next thing, sucked along by capillary action down a torrent of intensely demanding projects. Accelerating, in a sense, his future.

His body knew better than to talk to a man with his mind on other matters.

I was similar that way, with the lifetime supply of urgent missions. I knew firsthand how such projects could assume imposing magnitude, cut as they were from the whole cloth of the imagination, not always with proper scissors and in need of tailoring. His were serious, socially mindful projects that drew him completely into his brain, up, up, and away, where nothing and nobody else mattered.

It's almost as if he knew he'd one day need this skill my mother possessed, her amazing talent for zeroing in on impending illness, nipping flu in the bud, curing broken bones with boiled comfrey. This communion of body and mind was surely what my father hoped to learn from the *fakir* as I called him, a hokey trumped-up sad sack of a flim-flimming mystic Dad got mixed up with when I was

4

a teen, decades before the cancer diagnosis. He experimented with other clap-trapping purveyors of false wisdom whose shark-fins encircled our house, and those of his friends as well, but the fakir made the keenest impression on us all.

The key (said this fakir) to building a lasting mind-body bridge was faith. Unequivocal belief generated a one-pointed mental focus, he maintained, much as a magnifying glass gathering sun rays could produce fire. This one-pointed focus could alter the course of events, or if turned inward, clear up rashes, even strip out a tumor. It required the willingness, or whateverness, to believe things that didn't seem at *all* likely with the same inevitability with which you knew megachains would someday take over your downtown area. You mailed electric messages through your nervous system with conscious thoughts to them attached like price tags. Above all, you couldn't allow counteracting thoughts to intervene for an instant, thoughts like: "What if this doesn't fucking work?"

Those kinds of thoughts were my territory.

I'd have preferred a frank talk with my father after the diagnosis, but that would have marred his concentration and I could see he was busily trying to put into practice the techniques his various gurus and fakirs had emphasized.

My mother, playing interpreter, hastened to explain: "Try things Honey, sniff vitamins, check labels, see what strikes a chord."

Chord? My father squinted at her.

"Read books. Talk to herbalists or acupuncturists. Your body will tell you if they can help," my mother encouraged.

It was clear to me that her unbending determination created a placebo effect. Sheer bravado enhanced whatever treatments she undertook when ill, and wised up her immune system, rallying its happy little natural-killer cells.

5

There were times she'd clutch her head and retreat into darkness, migraine-leveled. "I'm fine," she'd say greenishly, but if I asked again later she'd be *honestly* fine. She never touched drugstore drugs. Although frankly her knee hadn't healed right, but we didn't discuss that.

"Experiment, Love!" she urged, smiling as she handed my father a tumbler of thick green juice. "You'll be drawn to healing sources. You'll just *know*." A sickening silence followed, during which we all stared at the green swamp juice.

"I'll just *know?*" my father bellowed. "I haven't just *known* anything my entire life! I don't *get* intuitive flashes of absolute holy conviction! It's all guesswork to me. It always has been!" he roared, prompting me to reflect, in an all-new light, upon the many road trips and trail hikes he'd commandeered during my formative years with such apparent bravado. "I... won't... just... *know*," he added quietly, starting to cough.

I wanted to run up and throw my arms around him right then but it wasn't our way.

Sometimes, in retrospect, everything matters much more than you allowed it to matter while it was actually happening. Or perhaps you didn't quite grasp what was in the works at the time, so you never got around to pondering the ramifications until they fell on your head. On the other hand, sometimes it's so much better not to grasp them. This was my mother's entire rationale for avoiding grim medical pronouncements. Bad news depresses people; depressed people get sicker. Clinical trials exist to demonstrate this, too.

The notebooks lay on a shelf in my father's study. I wasn't snooping, not yet anyway, for he hadn't been dead long, but underneath the manila folders my mother asked me to fetch were six notebooks, all different colors. The red one, I couldn't help noticing, dated back to the fakir era when I was fourteen.

6

At first my father droned on about his diet, or how often he meditated. Then my name appeared, along with strict injunctions from the fakir for my father to avoid me, much as it might pain him. Which it apparently did. For pages, and between the ruled lines, he deliberated in a soliloquy worthy of Hamlet. What he never once questioned in the course of this soul-searching was the twisted blarney the fakir handed him for a reason: father and daughter had reunited in this life thanks to a carnal bond in some previous incarnation. If my father didn't step away, we'd reenact our karma—a fate, apparently, worse than death.

Over the years from the time I left home for college, words flowed steadily between my father and me in a pattern like rain, neutral, unvarying, mainly in the back-ground. But when I drove down that last time, he looked so yellow and grimacing I couldn't stand aloof. He'd failed his own faith test, having neglected to will into being some alternate reality in which he was not dying of cancer. He hadn't managed to save the planet either, which shamed him horribly in addition to not being im-mortal. It was no wonder I had never quite made his grade.

I hugged him. "I wish I had a magic bullet for you, even a placebo one."

He threw me a quick bright smile that fell like a warm cape around my shoulders. "Placebo's good medicine," he said. "But you're better."

Then I found myself telling him in all sincerity that he hadn't failed a bit, hadn't failed me in my teens or my mother, but had really done his best, and had in fact accomplished many wonderful things and made scores of people very happy.

I saw the pain lift from his face as he inhaled these

words like a balm, and recalled that placebo means "I please." It's doubtful that I could have been so convincing had I read his notebooks *first*. Yet when I did read them, only weeks later, they made no difference.

I've seen healers. I've seen fakirs. I know good love from sick love, and no one can convince me otherwise, for that's what I believe unequivocally, with one-pointed focus, and so all is well.

The Acromegaly Man

"Gotta *work!* Gotta go to *work!* Everybody gotta WORK!" *I* hear coming down the street as I slave over my salvias. The approaching shape towers over the stunted street trees, but the man's upper spine, as if bent by the weight of his skull, forms a bony platform from which his head juts like an formidable, oddly-mounted hood ornament. "Gotta work!" He shouts with a friendly open-thumbed Gumby wave, still a block away. There's not another soul out. The crackhead who runs the daycare center next door isn't open for business today. The yuppies across the street are carpooling their long way home from Silicon Valley, and the sailboat's gone from the old man's driveway, which means he's out fishing in the Bay for another tritium-laden dinner.

I rip up clots of oxalis, bang the dirt off their sneaky roots, and smile up at the massive cranium blocking the late afternoon sun. Acromegaly does that, my husband the scientist claims. Surplus human growth hormone thickens the facial bones. The acromegaly man hovers approvingly as I stoop over the roses. "Gotta *work!*" His sad eyes bulge with the weight of the world, but his smile radiates genuine sweetness. "Bufull," he points at my clutter of flowers. We understand each other, he and I, just as the Chinese man who walks by each day with his four tiny kids under one giant parasol articulates his understanding of kids, death and roses perfectly without a word of English.

"Yup, gotta work!" I agree, convincingly enough that the acromegaly man seems cheered and continues his loose-limbed, cowboy squatwalk toward the busy corner where the day-hookers stand exactly a yard apart, each pretending to be alone.

"Gotta *work!*" he calls to them, raising a power fist just as he disappears around the corner onto San Pablo Avenue. I feel a squeeze of affection, wondering, as I dig a trench for the dutch iris, what the acromegaly man would say if I told him this garden's my playpen. It's my way to offset the newroom's jarring atmosphere, the hours running around the city photographing bleeding bodies and smashed storefronts, work I once—did I really?—yes, thrived on. Now it's the garden that thrives.

The acromegaly man has elephant ears, so the neighbors call him "Dumbo," but I'm sure his great skull conceals a superior if atypical brain, just as I'm certain the Chinese father was once an important leader, and that my crack-smoking neighbor leaves her daycare charges with a ten-year-old niece while she vanishes into bars. Just as everyone on the whole block knows my husband loves someone else. They may even know who.

Sure enough, the acromegaly man is right with it the next evening when I ask what his job is. "Night custodian, Bread Box," he replies instantly with a statesmanlike headshake, "Six to three-thirty I mop 'n' glow, comet, windex, pledge, palmolive!"

I nod knowledgeably.

"But ya gotta WORK!" he admonishes in a much harsher tone, beating his forefinger rather close to my face, his brow stern even as his eyes gather mist. He's told me before that he lives up the street with his parents. From the alien expression hardening his features, I suspect it's his father talking, his father's face, his father's phrase pounded into him daily.

My heart wilts. I snap off a fragrant rose—Double Delight, my favorite—and hand it to him. The acromegaly man gapes as if I've proposed to him. He takes the rose and races down the street with it cupped to his chest, as if he might be accused of stealing.

I've read that human growth hormone is a chemical people magically secrete which keeps our tissues young and can even cure wasting. He's got too much of a good thing. I can't help wondering if we all oversecrete some benign substance or other, some excess goodness we're forever at the mercy of.

The rainy season comes on full force and I don't see the acromegaly man for awhile. The garden turns yellow-leaved, breeding mushrooms shaped like ears raised just high enough above the soggy soil to eavesdrop. Only my princess tree glows, the garden's showpiece, thrusting out regal purple blooms jeweled with beads of deflected rain. After work I see friends, go to concerts, drive around until bedtime, so I won't have to come home and pretend I don't know why, no matter how late I come home, my husband will arrive later still.

He isn't in bed at 3:00 am when I'm called out to cover a drive-by. In a bar full of carnage I find four spent lives and a child who will never be a child again thrashing in the arms of an officer. She could be the crackhead's niece. In the darkroom, four faces emerge trapped in emulsion, four identities bound for the front page. I scissor up the proofs and half the negatives, printing only the blurred shots and two of covered gurneys.

"Your work's going to shit, Iris." The editor-in-chief tosses my prints down, flint-eyed. "Care to explain?" I can't. "One more botched job, and—" The hand across the throat.

It rains nonstop for days, wind shrieking ghoulishly. The morning the storm clears, I step outside. The princess tree has blown down, snapped at the base, its corpse lying full length across the sidewalk. Seven years, it took to gain such magnificence—the entire span of our marriage. I stand there blinking, then run inside, pack two suitcases and head for the door. My husband drains his coffee cup and follows, yelling questions I should be asking: "How can you think of throwing it all away?" I start up my car but he leaps on the hood, spreading his body across the windshield so I can't drive away without hearing him out. He'd never have tried that in the rain, I consider, noticing for the first time that he's grown a beard. "You never used to come home at decent hours," he objects, which I can't deny. I'm stunned when he says I've been so besotted with my camera, he had to bury himself in his own work in self-defense and he's decided he likes it that way.

Later as I pick pieces of princess tree off the sidewalk, I hear: "Gotta WORK!" The acromegaly man stops to gather an armful of fractured limbs, so tenderly he could be lifting an infant. He lingers. "Don't wanna work today," he whispers as if we share one sorrow. "Bob tries to hurt me. He pushes me on the floor-wax floor." He flashes a bruised elbow.

"Is Bob someone at the bakery?"

"Yeah! I gotta work. But Bob is bad. He wants me to fall." He glances fearfully at the princess tree.

"Bob IS bad," I agree. "Don't let him near you."

"I won't!" he promises. "Won't fall," with a grateful flick of smile that lets me imagine I've solved something. "Won't let him, near," he mutters, loping off.

Next I see him, he's anxious again. "Bob stole money, says I took it. No!"

I sprinkle snailbait by the crocus shoots and speak of workplace treachery.

"Thank you!" He pats my arm. "I didn't, didn't know why, what to do."

Every day there's a new Bob story. I fantasize about storming into the Bread Box to confront this demon. But I'm too ashamed. I can't confront my own.

I'm the acromegaly man's only confidante. "No one listens," he admits as I face the princess tree stump, framing it like a camera with both hands to help me conjure fresh

12

possibilities. Nothing suggests itself. There's no substitute for the royal purple splendor in my mind's eye, and I can't bear to start over. I pack up my tools and climb onto the porch. He trails behind: "Bob hides behind the door. There's a bucket, water on my head." I step inside the house, turning in the doorway to offer last-minute advice, but he cuts in. "Bu-full," he murmurs, suddenly very close. Huge, heavy arms surround my neck so that I fall into him, my face pressed into his bicep. His hug crushes the air from my lungs, I'm drowning in his nylon sleeve, and I panic and pummel him, hard. His grip slackens. I duck under his arm, fly through the house and sail out the back door.

But not before I see the look on his face. It's the same unquenchable dismay my husband telegraphs whenever I meet his gaze: I am Bob to him now.

Yes, I want to tell him. But so are you. We are all Bob.

It's not missing my garden so much as being cooped indoors, captive audience to the cacophony of howling dogs and children in the poor, addicted daycare teacher's backyard. It's not being cooped up so much as watching the acromegaly man pass by each afternoon, eyeing the garden, which has never been more colorful, exploding with spring bloom. I hear his distant cry: "Gotta work!" Yes, but sometimes...it just doesn't.

It has only been three days, but it's enough. My suitcase is waiting, the rain's stopped, my husband's at his job, and it no longer feels like any sacrifice at all to leave what I've invested here for others to enjoy or disparage as they will.

Horoscope

You're anything but aroused, but you rest your reporter's clipboard strategically across your lap as a precaution. "So...tell me what goes through your mind," you start off the interview, choking a bit on dressing-room talc suspended in the air, "when you march out onstage decked in that—" You break off again; what to call this tiny fringed scarlet thong-thing she's doing warm-ups in? Her can-canning legs send out dangerous dark flashes with every kick. You try not to stare at what was once sacred.

"What am I thinking? Oh, that I'm an angel," she says with a piercing smile, hardly angelic. You think of *The Blue Angel* and feel like a clown. "An angel...come to save the wicked from themselves!" She laughs at her own bullshit, shakes out her limbs, and straddles the stool next to yours, leaning into the bubble-lit makeup mirror to outline her lips in black.

You flinch as her elbow grazes yours. You *knew* you shouldn't have taken this assignment. Just couldn't resist.

"Seriously, I love the attention. Celebrity limos, flowers, gifts—and I never have to write thank-you notes!" She offers a slender hand in evidence, a hand that never writes thank-yous, though it's clearly capable of many things. In high school you held this hand for two years and considered yourself damn lucky: a gorgeous, popular babe with top grades. You were planning to get married. She said she was saving herself for you.

She's a national sex symbol now. A household name—to most men. A name usually seen on video boxes, but sometimes on marquees.

"Are there no regrets?" You grin tightly, showing your dimples and wagging a teasing moral finger. "Didn't

you once aspire to be a physician? Tell the truth, now."
Little sell-out! As if she'd ever been honest with you!

When you knocked on her dressing-room door a minute
ago, you honestly expected to see a strung-out, bony wreck, a
creature with tracks up her arms, blue bags under her eyes.
You came here for vindication. But she's tricked you again;
nine years haven't so much as smudged her small, unclouded
face, her milkmaid purity, that maddening victory smile.

"Well, no." She paints on shimmering purply-rose eye
shadow, demurely demonic. "Sometimes it's like...I'm asleep
in hell but I'm dreaming I'm in heaven. But I know I don't
have to wake up, at least not for a good long while."

Heaven and hell. You nod encouragingly. "You mean
hell's out there waiting?" you prompt. Her folks, you
recall, were strict Catholics. A good angle, though your
editor favors **Prom Queen to Porn Queen.** *You* find this
crude; you and your editor don't agree on much. You
suspect he'd love to can you, so you never mentioned that
you knew her from back home. Conflict of interest; it's
against the paper's rules.

She always said you lacked a reporter's cutthroat
instincts, didn't she?

"No, Bill," she says now, wearing a baffled look. "Hell's
not *waiting*." Hell's always out there, is all. You've gotta
banish it from your life like a bad relative. Learn to forget!"
She counsels as if you'd come for therapy. But she's right;
you're incapable of forgetting.

You remember all too well, for instance, how she
used to rail about the deliberate cruelty of "the Mother,"
her adoptive stepmother. She claimed the Mother made
up stories about her for the enjoyment of guests. When
she was a tiny thing, the Mother told visitors, she'd steal
a carton of eggs from the fridge when no one was looking
and stand at the top of the cellar stairs, tossing eggs one

by one down the concrete steps with a scream of glee at each explosion.

In high school you didn't believe that story, but you do now. You picture the eggs that are her children, strangling one by one in her IUD.

Somewhere a fuzzy, disembodied voice blares announcements.

"Whoa!" She leaps up. "Gotta get moving, it's almost time!" She dashes around the tiny room, throwing props in a twine-handled Macy's bag.

"Wait, we're not done. There's more I need to know!" you object, eyeing what goes into her bag: ostrich feathers, more thong-things, a huge comical dildo like those you've seen in catalogues, those whirring, mechanized sex toys you've never even tried. All you ever wanted were ordinary things: a devoted woman, a passel of kids, your byline on the front page. You've achieved only one of these.

"Don't worry, we'll finish up after the show. I got you a front row seat," she winks, slipping a trenchcoat over her scarlet lingerie.

Jesus. Now you'll have watch the whole show! Something snaps in your brain like a metal-fatigued paper clip. Of course—your editor would be apoplectic if you didn't see the act. And she'll ask how you liked it, you know she will.

She tosses on a fedora. "Some muckety-muck producer's in the audience, so I have to run along. I hope he enjoys himself. I could use the exposure!" Whirling in the doorway, she flaps open her trenchcoat to flash her red satin crotch. Like a toreador teasing a bull.

When she laughs this way, it really sounds like ha-ha-ha. You remember that too. How she used to laugh at all your jokes, slapping her thighs. It made you feel superior and you loved her all the more for that. She cried easily, too.

Time out, she'd whimper, hiding her wet face in cupped hands. When she went to blow her nose, you peeked under her pillow and found a Harlequin romance.

"See you after the show," she blows you a kiss from the doorway.

"How about a real kiss for an old friend?" you call out experimentally.

"We were high school sweethearts, Bill. Not friends." She gives you that taunting smile you used to think was a cover for shyness, and steps out into the hall. You quench a powerful impulse to grab her by the trenchcoat and shake her. What could you have done differently? You tried to be a nice guy! You accepted her virgin status with only minor protests. There were religious reasons; she wasn't ready to have her Harlequin scene blown. Still, your friends were rough on you. *Thweet William,* they called you. *Hey, Thweetyboy!*

She steps back into the dressing room: "I waited for you, you know."

"It sure doesn't look that way!"

"For a whole year after you left, I waited. For a letter, or a call. Anything." She vanishes. Seconds later, you hear a startling crash. You realize it's her fans—the explosion of applause out in the theatre that announces her arrival onstage. You stagger out into the audience, falling into the chair that's got your name taped to the back. Up onstage, she's still wearing that trenchcoat. But it won't be long.

The other men look like regulars. "Lucky guy!" A shriveled drunk cackles at you in a husk of a voice.

A young man, a mere *kid,* elbows you, leering. "That's the hot seat," he points at your chair and licks his lips. "She *loves* audience participation."

17

You should have known. Once again she's set you up. You sit there watching yourself sitting as if through a camera slowly panning away. You see yourself sitting on the front steps of your high school, young and eager, waiting to meet the college rep from a journalism school across the country. You're a senior peering into the crystal ball of your future and trying to read the horoscope written there in its murky depths, a senior with plenty on your mind: a girlfriend you adore who insists on preserving a tiny membrane, a girl who mocks your great ambition to be a news reporter though you're a hit at the school paper, who urges you not to go away, though there's no j-school for 500 miles. You imagine yourself getting up off those steps and walking away before the college rep arrives. For in fact you aren't sure you can go through life asking people questions about things you might rather not know.

But you didn't walk away back then; you stayed and met with the college rep, you signed the papers, you left her in her nunnery. So you get up and walk away now, as if finishing the act you never completed, the fate you didn't choose.

Even as she dances up there on stage, dangling her spangled crimson teddies on a finger, she spots you standing up in the tiny theatre, and waltzes down the promenade to intercept you, her eyes meeting yours over the footlights, accusing: *There you go again, tough guy, always leaving just when the show starts. Like you left me for J-school just when I'd set my heart on having you.*

The red bra flies off. You stop and stare, telegraphing your reply: *Then why always your fool, your rules, your terms?* You're mincing toward the nearby exit, still holding her gaze, knowing that with these few steps you're throwing away the interview and god knows, maybe your job. Her eyes are slits. You pass so close on your way to the exit, you fancy you can see right into her mind, as if this has all been said before: *No guts, Bill. You never stand and fight, expecting your rewards handed on a platter. You still don't understand that life is only*

     one

     l-o-n-g

     s-t-r-i-p-t-e-a-s-e.

You turn your back on her, veering toward the other exit, the one at the back with the red bar across the door that reads: **Caution: Alarm Will Sound** and you press that bar, hard, and walk straight through the clamor into fresh air, closing your eyes against the brightness.

You had completely forgotten that outside, it's still broad daylight.

Bad Habits

Every Thursday El comes to dinner, but she never fails to leave her husband at home. He was a Jesuit priest before she proposed to him—her third, most long-lived marriage—and when I was younger, I used to think El visited us by herself because she was afraid her husband would show up wearing his hairshirt. I should've known that nobody who's married to El would have any use for a hairshirt.

El herself wears shadow-colored dresses that cling to her bony body, ebony maroons, foresty earthtones which accentuate the parts of her still thirsting for mistletoe kisses and sequin-studded evenings at the theatre. She makes a certain statement by not coloring her hair. But then she still looks a good decade younger than my mother, who roomed with her in college. El and my father got along famously then. They were a tight trio. The real reason El leaves her husband at home is so that she can return to the enchanted isle of the past where she and my parents were young and brilliant together.

"Could you please pass the salt?" I ask her nicely at dinner.

"Sodium bloats you," she says, in a tone that makes it personal. I'm in the way, to be blunt, just as her husband would be if he came along. El wouldn't mind at all if I'd never been born. My existence plays havoc with her delusions. "Don't you have term papers to write, Maddie?" she quips when I try to join the dinner conversation, as if participating were an impertinence on my part. She cuts me off in mid-sentence, refers to my vintage clothing as "rags," mentions that I still live at home every chance she gets.

The allure she holds for my parents mystifies me. I've asked my mother for photos of their trio from the old days, but she says she can't find any. So I try to imagine that three-way friendship, hours of animated French chatter at the mug n' muffin place in Brattle Square, nights of devout suffering over calculus in the library, boat races, picnics by the Charles. Nothing helps. El will always be the fiend who tore my flamenco dancer costume under the pretense of admiring it, scarring its red satin bodice the night before I starred as Carmen in the school play. ("Forgive her, Maddie, she's envious."). So what was it about El that so bewitched my parents? The praise she heaped on my father's dissertation? Or was it the way she used to tug down my mother's dress in the back to hide the frill of her slip as they left the dorm for a mixer?

Over dinner, El lectures us about middle age (pinching her brow at me, the college girl, as if to confirm youth is wasted on the young), how midlife is the best time in a woman's life, a blast of alpine freshness after the hot driven angst of youth. El's made a quite a name for herself with these truisms in a popular vein of women's psychology and self-help books. Her sales quadruple my father's, though he's written more books. He coughs a lot when El visits, forgets to finish sentences. She comforts him gravely, hunching over her salad as if to pay homage to a dead religion. "Academic writing is so underappreciated." Ha, I think; El's waited decades for this chance to get back at my father for never sleeping with her. I know she sleeps with everyone else's husband.

Or rather I should say, she *used* to. Past tense. I can't seem to get it through my skull that El is dead, dead and gone. Funny, how it slips my mind. I'm so used to hating her it's become a habit, and habits know no season; they're not as fragile or as mutable as real events. True, El's been gone only a month. Still, you'd think her violent demise would hang around my neck like a bag of bricks. Because in my childish heart, I often prayed for her death. And I wanted it to hurt, badly, as she'd pained me all these years.

You think I'm a beast, I know. I got my vicious wish, you'll say. Am I satisfied now with my petty revenge? El's history. I have a whole life ahead.

Believe, though, I never envisioned so cruel a fate, not even for El. A fall like that, a fall from grace! I even cried along with my mother from the sheer shock of it, El's name splattered across the headlines. We read them together, me resting my hand on my mother's shaking shoulder; she, comforted only by the thought that it was better for El to go out in a blaze like some comet than to wither in the crust of old age like ordinary mortals. I'm sorry for El. But I'm not sorry she's gone.

Though I have regrets, deep regrets. I need to miss her, or something about her, this frequent, loved guest of my family. I comb memory, scrutinizing every detail of that last night El came to dinner, looking for something to love so I can feel human again.

And there she is, the instant I shut my eyes, aggressively alive in a floor-length black velvet cape and smoky crepe dress. The tinkle of her earrings is maddening as she waltzes in our front door, reeking of lilies. Already she has made a bad start, no endearing, redeeming qualities in sight. She's two hours late to dinner, and hasn't even called. My father and I are famished, cranky. The overdone roast is cold. I glower at my mother when the doorbell finally rings and she dashes for it, shushing me:

"Easy, Maddie. I'm sure there's a good reason. Maybe she and Ron had a fight."

I hang back in fury as my mother hugs El in the front hall. Then we sit at the table eating the soufflé my mother whipped up to replace the roast. My father and I wolf it off our plates in slabs. Even my mother's small bites are eager, peckish. But El picks greens from her soufflé, eats only those. She makes her pitches about how much she's enjoying her "prime," interrupting herself to grab my hand with the fork still in it.

"Don't eat so fast, Maddie. It's bad for your digestion—not to mention your figure." She holds my hand in a vise-grip. "Don't you want to be asked out on dates?" She crushes my fingers so I want to yelp, to shriek in her ear, throw dishes, slap her face. I want to insist that I get plenty of dates without starving myself to a shadow. But this will only make me appear whiny and childish. Which is exactly what El wants.

After dinner, El coaxes my mother into the living room for the usual chat. She never includes me on these occasions, just tucks my mother's hand girlishly under her arm as she rises from the table and leads her away. Will she tell my mother of some new twist in her mysterious marriage, some sexual thrill she thinks my mom should try out? I'm no child, I remind myself, no virgin either. I'm graduating from college soon. My mother won't mind if I join them. She's always yearned for me and El to get along. So I break the taboo, leave the dishes, and knowing El won't welcome my company, follow them out of the kitchen. My father stays at the table reading and doesn't even look up.

In the living room, El grabs the only plush armchair, leans back, legs crossed stylishly, jiggling her steaming coffee. I bet she wishes she had a vodka tonic instead. I wouldn't mind one myself, but my parents don't drink. El veers the conversation toward me, mimicking the behavior of a polite guest for my mother's benefit.

"So, Maddie, you're graduating! Tell us your plans."

I'm wary; she's constantly setting me up to fall on my face. Then I see her scratch her thigh in an undignified spot, and realize she's unaware of herself at this moment; her smile reaches for me, stretching as far as it can, like someone leaning perilously from a balcony. She's trying, the best she can, asking me to meet her halfway.

I consider reaching out across the gulf between us. Can I trust her not to drop me? I don't. "I let my plans evolve," I tell her, "I don't *make* plans. What I actually do with my life isn't important to me as long as I'm happy." I don't mean this.

"True," El's voice speeds up. "Happiness isn't a formula, but you must work at it. You won't find it sitting around your parents' house waiting for you!" Her glance sidles cautiously to my mother's face, checking, then flicks back at me. I turn from her gaze.

My mother bites her lower lip. She has slipped off her shoes because they pinch, and her bare, red feet snuggle each other for comfort under her chair. El snaps her fingers and jumps up to get something, an old snapshot. "Lost for decades in the frame behind another photo," El explains. I'm mildly touched. She's not only remembered my desire to see a photo of the trio, but granted it. We huddle; there are my young parents, spiffy in formal attire, my father dark and wetted down, my mother pale and fluffed up. There is El and a pretty dark-haired boy with an enraged smile. El's decked in a rosecolored gown and sparkling tiara that would make anyone less radiant look clownish.

"God, El!" I cry, caught up in her loveliness, "What a knockout you were!" This is my concession for the evening, my contribution to good will, my token kindness.

But when I look at El, I see anguish twisting in her face, an injury I didn't intend.

"Oh, and you still are!" my mother quickly assures her, but the damage is done.

"That shot was taken at our graduation ball, wasn't it?" El says in a cross, quaky old-lady voice. "What a splendid night that was! Too bad you'll miss out on the fanfare, Maddie," she says. "Your state college ceremony won't be much." Under her chair, the many eyes of El's fishnet stockings wink as she shifts her legs. She brings the coffee cup to her lips, pretends to sip, but her throat doesn't move. My mother looks close to tears.

24

"I don't think I'd have fit in at Radcliffe anyway, El." I say pointedly. "Do you?" I get up and head for the door, because I figure I may as well go and do the dishes now.

As I stalk off, El says loudly to my mother, "Maddie's going to be one of those women like me, who are happier when they're older." Her thin hands flutter, and she grips the arms of her chair, almost feebly, for balance. When I see that gesture, I realize that El, like me, is nervous. Like me, she's probably dying for a cigarette—I've seen the pack in her purse, my brand—but my mother is under the impression El quit that foolish habit eons ago, and El doesn't want to disillusion her. Nor do I. My mother would be hideously disappointed in me. So I only smoke on the deck at night when no one's up.

Those fluttering hands are the last I ever see of El. But what, I wonder, might have happened if my mother had been called away by her pager that night and if El and I had stepped out on the deck together to indulge our wicked vices? Perhaps we'd have fought like hens. I might've been tempted to shove her over the railing, as her Jesuit husband finally did during one of their fights, in a terrible culmination of passionate rage. And yet somehow I believe that if my mother and father hadn't been there, El would have pulled out her pocket flask and offered it to me, and we'd have puffed away at our cigarettes on the deck and talked, talked about all the men we'd slept with and the ones we wanted to sleep with, and all the places we wanted to go and what we wanted to do there, and what it was like to feel old when you were young and young when you were old, and how most of all it was hard to be satisfied with the things you had, because no matter what, you always wanted more.

Ouija

Her name was Ouida, but in fifth grade no one could conceive of a name like that, based in ancient history (another classmate, Bede-the-less-than-honorable, was "Beady Eyes"), so Ouida became "Weedy" and later, "Ouija."

About that time, not entirely by coincidence, I discovered that we did not have a Ouija board in our house, nor would we ever harbor such "hokum" as my mother put it, inside the Corinthian columns and oaken frontiers of our gracious home.

Oh.

I walked to the bus stop every day with three other girls and soon found out that Torrie and Patty both had Ouija boards. Ouija was based on the wisdom of ancient East Indian spirits called back from the dead, they said, or Pythagoras or something like that, and I could come play with it anytime I wanted, but really, it was no more exciting than Magic 8-ball.

Yawn.

I might have forgotten all about it if Ouida hadn't shadowed me the next day after school as I raced for the bus. I was one of those perpetually tardy kids, always a step behind, not because I was especially slow but because I actually stayed to finish things. That day I'd finished a linoleum block print of palm trees and hula dancers I'd been working on in Art, little knowing I'd pay for my perfectionism with multiple bruises. I capped the inks and ran as hard as I could after the departing school bus until it rounded the corner, poofing black diesel smoke. I paused at the curb to consider my options. The next thing I knew I was lying in the gutter while Ouida stomped on my collarbone and straddled my breathless body, pounding it with all her might.

Finally I grabbed her pantleg, toppled her, and raced off down the street.

I flagged a cab and gave Patty's address, where I went to lick my wounds before going off to survey the wreckage at home. Patty and I set up her Ouija board on the red Turkish carpet in her living room. My idea was that Ouija would tell me what to do in revenge for Ouida's surprise attack. She was a known bully but I had, up until then, considered myself too well connected to be a target. Should I tie her up, all smeared with molasses, and leave her on an anthill? Maybe I could distribute a rumor that she had crab lice from molesting the janitors. The life of an urban school child is full of such information.

Patty and I knelt by the Ouija board holding hands, and let the indicator move freely over the wooden board. The question of What to Do About Ouida was swiftly answered, so swiftly I felt a chill. Patty stared at me with her perfectly round brown cow-eyes as wide open as they'd go. The Ouija board had formed the words:

BE KIND

"What?" I screeched, outraged. "How's that supposed to help?"

"Maybe it's in your best interests?" squeaked Patty.

Ouida was twice as big as any of us, probably older and held back a few grades.

"Let's try it again!" I said. "Close your eyes this time." I suspected Patty of being a dyed-in-the-wool pacifist. She did not seem to be exerting any special effort, however. I watched her the whole time.

B-E K-I-N-D, Ouija spelled out again.

It was *so* not my day. I decided I might as well go home and face the opera music, probably La Traviata since it was Monday and my mother was usually in a dramatic drunk on Mondays. As opposed to Tuesdays or Thursdays, when she taught all morning and was normally in more of a dead stupor when I got home. My father claimed to live here and travel frequently on business, but I felt he lived on the road, carefree, and only home was work to him.

In fact, Mom was playing Mozart that day, the intro to the Magic Flute, one of her more tolerable recordings. She was not so far gone that she didn't notice the purple lump Ouida had made of my cheek.

"Beth, what have you done to yourself?" my mother demanded, rushing at me so that I leapt away in alarm. "Did you start a fight?"

Aren't you starting one? I wanted to say. But I'd learned to take the shortest route with my mother, always, unless my father was home on one of his rare visits. So for expediency's sake, I told her I'd attempted a prodigious gymnastics stunt that hadn't quite worked out and she said she completely understood.

"It's important that you tried, Beth! That's what counts," she said hugging me tightly around the ribs.

Ow.

But she didn't give hugs very often, so I submitted. She behaved herself for the rest of the evening, too, acting reasonably cheerful, offering to make whatever I wanted for dinner. She didn't make any weird comments when I went to bed early without eating much, either. It always seemed better, in the long run, to find ways to please or console her than to defend myself directly.

Ouida haunted me at school the next day. Surprise! I evaded her all morning, but she caught me alone on the landing at lunchtime when the classroom door was locked and the teacher wasn't around. I knew I couldn't beat her in a fistfight, and if I said anything sassy, she'd go for right for my throat. If I sounded too sweet and cajoling, she wouldn't buy it. There weren't many options and she was circling around me, getting closer with that weird flat look in her eye. They didn't make people like her in glossy, only matte.

Maybe the Ouija board had a point. I thought about how well it had worked, coping with my mother the night before by trying to be nice to her. Did the dead know better than we? Was I about to join them? My heart raced. I made sure Ouida was between me and the staircase.

"Ouida, someone must be doing something pretty bad to you, if you don't even think twice about jumping a perfect stranger," I said as calmly as I could. She gave me a blank stare. "Most people only hit people they *know*." I shook my head and walked toward the stairs, ready to breathe my last. "Maybe you should tell someone." To my amazement, Ouida didn't block my path. I watched her from the corner of my eye and she didn't budge. She looked as if I'd hit *her*. I was clueless.

Magic!

I raced back to the playground and collapsed on a bench next to Torrie and Jill.

No way! They didn't believe me.

But a few minutes later, Ouida came stumbling by with her eyes on the ground.

She didn't give us a glance.

"What did you do to her?"

"Hexed her," I shrugged. I knew I'd scared her, but god-only-knows how.

Dad was supposed to come home that night for a week's layover, but he didn't show up and the phone was silent. By the time dinner was over (set with candles and a vase of fresh delphinium) my mother was too drunk to stand up on the first two tries. On the third try, she lurched to her feet, cracked her shin on the table leg, and started swearing.

"Stop!" I ordered. "I'll put the dinner stuff away. Just go to bed."

"Look at you! Bossy little fool. You're a mess. Who'd want to come home to this?" My mother picked up her wine glass and threw it. It shattered on the handpainted tiles, the colorful birds and flowers she'd had specially put in at the threshold to the kitchen.

"Good job!" I wasn't feeling too charitable. "How're you gonna feel if he walks in right now and sees all this glass, huh?" I egged her on coldly.

"Don't lecture me, Beth!"

"It's not my fault he doesn't love you!" I think this was a line from some movie I'd just seen. It had sounded good on screen, but my words echoed off the tiles like a curse.

She looked at me from the farthest corner of her eye and the darkest reaches of her heart.

"Mom, I'm sorry I said that."

She rushed at me, whacking and whaling away until I slipped out of her grasp. The next morning I was sore all over. I left before she woke up.

At school I called some numbers and reported her. She'd never lost it like that before. I didn't know what else to do.

By the time I got home from school, my dad was there, along the police and a social worker. My mother was sitting in the corner crying. She looked like she'd been crying all day. When I tried to go over and see if she was okay, the social worker pulled me aside and said it wouldn't be a good idea to talk to her right now.

I didn't see her for a year. The whole time I felt like the meanest person on earth.

During that year, I also found out that Ouija really wasn't based on anything ancient or mystical. It wasn't spirits communicating from the dead, just some good old

19th century spiritualists on a lark. I deduced that "be kind" was not any sort of imperative from the Great Beyond.

After I went to live with my father, I thought no one would ever hurt me again. I got to stay in a nice apartment in my own room with a canopy bed in a much livelier part of town, and go to a different school where there weren't too many bullies, and kids finished their schoolwork.

Soon after I moved there, my father began bringing home a woman, and not long after that, this woman became my stepmother. My stepmother made it her business to keep me from "bothering" my father when he was trying to relax, that is, whenever he was home and available. Any comment I addressed to him at the table, she intercepted and replied to. If he called on the phone, she grabbed the receiver away. If she knew I liked a certain kind of cereal, it would vanish from the shelf and be taken off the grocery list. If she knew I hated a dish, she'd serve it two or three times a week. She wouldn't stop talking long enough for anyone else to complete a sentence. My father was not exempt from this. In fact she often yelled at him at the top of her lungs, offering a smorgasbord of criticism. He didn't even blink. I got the impression he rather liked being ordered around. What else did this woman have over my mother?

I quickly stopped volunteering information about my preferences and dislikes, prompting my stepmother to follow me from room to room, even into the bathroom. If I asked for the privacy most people would expect, she blew up in my face. She rummaged through my drawers when I was at school, and didn't even slide them back in after she finished spying. It was no good complaining to my father, since I never had thirty seconds alone with him.

I tried everything to get along with my stepmother, and since she's still married to my father to this day, I'm still trying. Mostly I've tried kindness, knowing it won't change her behavior. It does not bring out native warmth, or make someone stop and think. Kindness can't be given with the expectation that it'll be reciprocated. I've even wondered if meeting meanness with kindness legitimizes and fosters meanness.

Is it mean to feel kindness as a burden? My stepmother can't help that, as a child, she narrowly escaped the Nazis and was bundled on the *kindertransport,* never to be re-united with her own family again. Moving from stranger to stranger, she never learned to speak the language of kindness. Whose burden is it, then? Ouija can't tell me. But for me to speak her language and behave in kind would be unkind, and that's a burden I'd have to own.

When my mother completed her year of treatment, I went back to live with her for the rest of my school days and was infinitely more tolerant of her foibles. She told me it had been tough, but she was glad she'd finally been forced to confront her drinking problem and she forgave me everything.

My senior year of high school, I noticed someone familiar-looking in my history class. Ouida. She'd become an honor roll student. As it turned out she was merely big for her age, not stupid, and had never been held back a single grade. She'd even lost the sullen, flat look in her eyes and was almost glossy.

"I remember you!" She smiled and came up to me. She looked excited to see me, in fact. "You said something to me once, back in elementary, I can't remember exactly what, but it was like you saw right into my soul. It scared the shit out of me. I had to figure out what you'd seen."

"Really?" I slid into the desk across the aisle and smiled back. "I don't remember." I figured, why call up the ancient spirits of the past?

Alpenglow

Hotel Alpenrose, read the caption under a glossy photo of a Swiss-style chalet with neat windowboxes ablaze in scarlet bloom, casting a rosy glow over snowcaps in the background standing tall and spiky as beaten eggwhites. "Alpenglow," Erika said aloud to no one, digging the phone out from under stacks of travel guides: alpenglow, one of those natural wonders like the aurora borealis she swore she'd see during her lifetime if it killed her. It was an impulse buy, but she dialed the travel agent and booked a double for four nights in May. "Pricey!" the agent pointed out brightly, as if a little bird had told her the fate of every penny was hugely debated in this household.

But last night out of the blue, Rich had announced that his new practice was booming, and insisted they splurge on what he called "our long-delayed honeymoon," as if their real honeymoon, two sleepless nights in a mosquito-infested American River cabin, hadn't really counted. Splurge? Erica was speechless; perhaps he'd meant to surprise her with the good news? Just that day she'd passed up a chance to buy cheap season opera tickets, certain he'd object. And she treasured the memory of those two sweaty river nights, the glassless window of their rotting honeymoon cabin suspended over rapids, Rich's arms around her waist tethering her as she leaned, fascinated, over the thrashing white water. Of course, she'd been someone else back then, someone she actually liked. A live wire, a Juilliard graduate, an avid reader, a mountain climber. If she'd seen the future from that paneless window, she'd never have believed how boring the next five years would be, working the world's dumbest desk job to get Rich through med school so he could be a cardiologist. She still hardly recognized this moonfaced

Erika in the mirror, auburn ringlets corporate-cropped in a shag like those 60s bathing caps that simulated puckish hair. Too many days she'd sat at that boxy desk juggling the phone as she typed, morphing into this dull creature, her fluid pianist's fingers turning to wooden dowels, neck muscles twisted in macrame knots, forcing cheer into her voice while her nerves flamed. She willed her senses to play dead since they failed to bring pleasure anymore, even the chocolates she stashed in her pencil tray a futile talisman against the fluorescent-lit tension followed by long nights alone while Rich did rotations. All this, so she could give a travel agent their credit card number without adding up the charges first!

When May came, Rich steered their rented Ford Fiesta out of Munich airport into a blaze of spring sunshine. With Chopin preludes playing on the tape deck, Erika watched dim highrise apartments give way to cobbled streets, then to lush, dandelion dotted fields rushing by on either side of the Autobahn, each new scene instantly thrust behind them into the past. She'd typed her last hateful memo a week before; the present was all churches with gilded cupolas and glockenspiels, farmhouses ringed with red tulips like Wagnerian fire. Did she dare look ahead at the future? She did, and found it good: two weeks of alp-climbing, then Paris. Fresh air, fine food, opera, romance. "Grape?" She dangled the fruit she'd bought in Munich to Rich's lips as he drove, but he turned his head, intently steering the car around a spiraling turn that clung to the mountain tightly as an apple peeled all of a piece. When they returned to Sacramento, she sighed, she'd teach piano again, audition for chamber groups, start a family with what she suspected were her few remaining eggs.

It was dusk in the Bavarian Alps as they approached the *Alpenrose* in a tiny toy town spread at the feet of an alp, like the miniature model villages in train stations.

Above the churchspire, peaks loomed mantled in ice, hemming in the buildings below like a bowl. Erika shivered. No tulips here. "We've gone back in time. It's still winter," Rich spoke her mind. "Maybe we can ski instead of hike." She nodded without agreeing. Even in the lowlands of the village, patches of crusty snow lay about like escaped laundry, sheets blown behind churches, panties snagged on the stone cornices of banks.

The *Alpenrose* was as charming as she'd hoped: hand-carved gables lacy as a child's paper snowflake, satin sachets and mints in china dishes set about the room, a great roaring fire in the walk-in stone fireplace of the dining hall. There were no scarlet flowers blooming, but after dinner Erika luxuriated in the jacuzzi and then, still wrapped in her towel, flopped down on their soft woven bedspread beside Rich. He lay facing the TV, watching a young Liz Taylor fan herself at a vanity, wearing only a slip and speaking a deep, laden German so out of synch with her gestures and character, Erika's skin crawled. Rich knew even less German than Erika, whose sparse vocabulary came from singing *lieder* but still he seemed spellbound by the badly dubbed drama.

"Hey." Erika slid her bare calf lightly along the top of his thigh. He patted her leg without shifting his gaze from the screen. She jerked her calf away and rolled onto her stomach, flipping the pages of a travel brochure filled with sun-baked scenes of Italy, terracotta and blue sky. She turned up the steam heat and sipped a tiny bottle of brandy she'd lifted from the airline, waiting. In the alley below their window, a man and woman carried on a conversation in German, voices rising in intensity, then tapering to murmurs.

"Hey Richie," Erika waved her garish brochure in his face. "What if we spent a couple days on the *Italian* side of the Alps? It'd be springtime there."

He glanced from the TV to her long enough to smile. "Whatever you like. It's your trip!"

Her trip? *It's your baby,* she could imagine him saying someday when she announced she was pregnant. Maybe that wasn't fair. He had so many life-and-death judgement calls in the operating room. Decisions, even recreational ones, seemed to oppress him. "If we go to Italy, we'll have to forfeit three nights here. The *Alpenrose* doesn't give refunds," Erika added, fully expecting Rich to overrule such wasteful plans.

"Sure, that's all right." Rich shifted on the bedpillows, yawning. Erika stared at him. The voices of the German couple in the alley grew loud, insistent, talking over one other in bursts.

"I'll plan out our new route, then." Erika crackled open the road map fiercely, popped another brandy, and located a nice direct route over the Alps into Italy, tracing the roads in red marker. She'd never consulted tourist agencies in her adventurous days, why now? She preferred uncharted paths where mysteries lay waiting to be solved. In Italy, which she only knew from pictures, there would be white marble palaces, paintings of madonnas in dim halls. She stared so hard at a shot of a sunny Italian lake that its rippled surface undulated.

She raised her head and rubbed her cheek. The bed-spread had left a ribbed imprint on her face and a dream was vanishing around a corner in her mind, gone but for a feeling that she'd been somewhere thrilling and wasn't happy to be back. Rich lay beside her asleep on his back in t-shirt and boxers, big feet flopping outward, the TV flickering in his glasses. Erika slid her hand down the cool plane of his thigh where the hair grew blond and fine into the crease of his groin, but he balled up on his side like a hedgehog, mumbling about jet lag. She stood, punched off the TV with her big toe, and clicked out the lamp. With the TV off, the voices of the German couple still arguing in the alley pervaded the room like an odor. She'd become used to the voices, imagining that she knew what they were saying. They were discussing a disagreement they'd tried to work out many times before, an impasse between them.

She crushed herself against Rich's back, but he didn't stir. She too was worn out, drained to the point of exhilaration. Fatigue twinged behind her eyeballs, pulsing in her kneecaps. She curved an arm around Rich's waist. Though his ribs stuck out sharply, his stomach ballooned under her hand, drum-tight. The dinner he'd ordered was outrageous: appetizers, three meat courses, potatoes, stew, salad, wine, pastry. No wonder he'd fallen into a stupor. "Live it up," he'd toasted her, but she hadn't lifted her glass.

Outside, the German man pleaded with tears in his voice as he made absurd promises to his lover, idealistic promises he'd never keep. Still, he meant them now.

A different man's voice broke in—a deep, aggressive bark delivering some harsh ultimatum. Erika sat up in bed as if someone had called her name. Three voices erupted at once. Then came a distinct thud and a woman's shrill cry. Erika rushed to the window. As she struggled to unlatch the complicated folding shutters she heard Rich say, "Go back to sleep, honey. It's just some drunk kids."

Erika was startled. His voice came through so distinctly from the bed it was as if he'd never been asleep at all. But then she thought how coherent he sounded when he answered dawn emergency calls at home. Yet he had no recollection of them the next day unless he'd actually had to get up, go out and do surgery.

"But someone's hurt," she whispered to the doctor in him.

Rich didn't answer, deep in his dreams again. Erika flung the shutters wide and pressed herself into the bench-like recess of the sill. Cold brick bit the fronts of her bare thighs as she leaned out over the alley. Directly below, a woman, a mass of dark hair in the lamplight, bent over a man sprawled on the ground, her shoulders quaking as she tried to revive him. The other man had gone. Erika didn't think of herself as spying; she knew this couple intimately, cared deeply for their welfare as for her own. She again considered waking Rich for medical aid. But the dark room behind her seemed to have floated away like a boat untethered from the dock while her back was turned—and Rich with it.

To her relief, the injured man sat up. His dark-haired lover helped him stand, her arm binding his waist as they rose in one body like runners in a three-legged race. Erika's big brother Tom had helped her up once, in just that way, after she'd fallen practicing toe loops at the ice-rink. One moment she'd been spinning through the air; the next, her older brother was leaning over her, his warm palm gently patting her cheek. Tom was a bully then, a constant source of aggravation, but when she saw his face bent over hers, his eyes all watery and scared, she'd understood for the first time that he loved her. He was governed by strange rules, unfathomable ones beyond his control, but she could see that her fall had afforded him, by these same rules, a chance to help, to wipe her tears on his sleeve, buy her cocoa from the Automat, and that he was glad for the opportunity. Nonetheless, it was disappointing when he'd punched her for no reason the very next morning. She felt much the same at this moment, watching the German couple limp away. Frozen as she was, naked by the window, she watched with a sinking heart until they'd completely vanished, delaying the moment when she'd have to turn and face the dark bedroom again.

She couldn't sleep all night. In the morning, she dozed fitfully, pleading jet lag as Rich drove. It was her turn, but he insisted he didn't mind, faithfully following the red line she'd drawn on the map the night before through more toylike towns with crocus-edged village greens, toward the alpine pass into Italy. At noon they ate hot pastrami at a tavern, laughing over the poodle-crazed proprietress, her dogs rushing around her feet so she could hardly balance a tray. Rich and Erika's heads touched at the table as they pointed out this or that doggie award to each other on the plaque-studded walls, mounted in amongst rusty implements of war.

They drove on, sunlight filling the car as Erika, filled with food, slept comfortably in a suspended state without dreams or thought, aware only of the car's steep slant as they ascended the foothills of one of the highest mountain ranges in the world. When she next woke, the sun had dipped almost below the heaps of snow piled high on the shoulders of the road. They entered a tiny hamlet, a few sunken A-frame houses and an inn announcing vacancy. "Nice to be off the beaten track, eh? No reservations required," Rich quipped, though he didn't slow down as it was still early to stop for the night. Erika didn't see a soul as Rich coasted through town.

The road narrowed to one lane as they continued climbing, until the snow bank grazed Erika's window on the turns. What if they met a car coming from the opposite direction? But it had been awhile since she'd seen a car coming the other way. A terrible suspicion awoke in her. She glanced at Rich, biting her lip but he drove confidently on. Should she say something? Icy lethargy settled over her body, from the heavy food, perhaps. Rich was a smart guy, a brilliant cardiac surgeon for christsakes, with a practice that took off like a shot. He could see matters for himself. In a few minutes surely he would. Why should she always be the one to cast a shadow on the day, breathing words of caution when that was not her way? She was an adventurer, someone who followed through, got to the bottom of the mystery, and never turned back until she did.

She shut her eyes as if to sleep, and must really have drifted off. When she opened her eyes again, all she could see was white. At first she thought they'd gone off the road and plunged into the snow bank. Dead ahead, a solid white wall rose up a few feet in front of the windscreen, eighty or ninety sheer vertical feet of solid ice. She was alone in the car. Rich in his red windbreaker stood looking very tiny at the point where the road dead-ended, the last patch of pavement simply vanishing beneath the vast white wall, which only grew higher as Erika craned her neck to gaze upward. What she'd taken at first for miniature Christmas trees balanced at the crest of the sheer wall she now realized were the tops of enormous pines, entirely swallowed but for their very tips in snow.

Rich was wild-eyed as he raced back to the car. "It'll be night soon!" The sun was poised at the brink of the wall, streaming dark amber light. Rich started the engine and tried to turn the car around, violently cranking the steering wheel as if he meant to unscrew it. "We've gotta get back to that village we passed an hour ago!" he cried, backing and filling frantically. The wheels spun as the car lodged itself deeply in the white mounds surrounding them on three sides. "Oh my god, we're stuck!" Rich beat his fists on the steering wheel.

"We'll be ok," Erika answered calmly.

Rich snatched up the windshield scraper, a cheap blue plastic thing like a child's beach shovel that had come with the rented car. "Help me dig us out before we freeze!"

40

Erika got out, hunting for a suitable tool. Scrabbling at the snow bank, Rich tried to dig the left fender free with the plastic scraper. He looked so silly in his childish red windbreaker, trying to move a mountain with a toy shovel, that she collapsed on her knees in the snow laughing. A light snow began falling, big, soft, spinning white disks many inches apart hurtling into their eyelashes.

"What's wrong with you? Don't you see we're in a fix?" he screamed, his face mottled with red—Rich, who never yelled, never got visibly angry or even ruffled, no matter how upset Erika became. She certainly had his attention now. "We could be caught in an avalanche! Don't sit there like an idiot! Help me!" Why was he chastising her, when he should have backed the car out straight, instead of trying to turn around in a confined space? She would drive once they freed the wheels; it would be no problem, though she'd have to drive in reverse for some distance. He was simply too flustered to manage it.

Erika unscrewed the plastic cup from the thermos and used it to scoop snow away from the back bumper. But each time she glanced at Rich flapping around with his toy shovel, she fell over laughing. The thought of the *Alpenrose*, all paid for with its fire blazing on the giant hearth, was ludicrous—she shook with mirth until her ribs felt spongy. The sun fell behind the white wall. She thought of the red line on the map and her brother's voice came back to her, mocking her favorite childhood movie *The Sound of Music* because, he said, the Von Trapps couldn't have escaped over the alps in just their concert frocks at any season.

"Are you nuts?" Rich wrenched her to her feet and shook her as another wave of laughter wracked her body. She tried to be serious, pretending he was speaking German like Liz Taylor and that helped sober her a bit, until he shouted, "Don't you even *care?*" in an ironic echo of herself all these past years. Then she fell to her knees again, doubling over. The snow stung her face and the wind fried her ears, but Rich was too much, and she never doubted they'd have the car free momentarily and be on their way.

Meanwhile, the unseen setting sun had inflamed the huge white world in rose neon, a flamingo pink, twittering aliveness infusing even the swirling flakes with a light lovelier than music. She stopped digging to gaze at the alpenglow. She wasn't going to let him ruin it for her: a promise fulfilled, a promise that for once in her life, didn't disappoint her.

"Don't you see, Erika?" Rich's voice cracked. "We could die out here!"

That only set her off laughing again. For honestly she couldn't remember a time when she'd ever felt so alive.

Sins of Omission

You keep asking about the drawings, but I'm telling you, they had nothing to do with it. Yes, really! Well, of course I drew those pictures of Oliver and Susan. But I'm only a witness. I'm a weak soul but I never hurt a fly. I can't claim any special powers. Jehovah in his wisdom does what's right and fair, that's all I know. They say that those He blesses receive eternal life, and I'm finally convinced, now that I've seen it for myself.

Okay, I'll explain about the drawings. But first, you have to understand what happened earlier. What that day was like! June 3rd, that's right—I remember it was the Sunday before finals and the whole dorm was in study mode. Everybody cramming except me. The communal kitchen reeked of coffee. The old gabled white cape that passed for a dorm was so quiet I heard clocks ticking I hadn't even noticed before. Oliver and Susan had taken over the sun porch for the day, sitting in full view of my window with all their textbooks and notepads and snacks piled around them on the old crates we used as tables out there. That porch was the nicest spot in the house, with screens instead of walls so you could be inside and outside both at once. In June the porch was heavenly, all honeyed with sweet peas and early corn swishing in the breeze.

My room had the only view of that sun porch. If I crouched by my window and looked down at a steep angle, I could see Oliver's profile through the screens, slouched in the battered gold velvet armchair we kept out there, his elegant black curls dripping off the headrest. I had the feeling he knew how gorgeous they looked against the gold velvet and hoped I was watching. I know he got a thrill from touching her in front of me. That's what makes what they did so bad—salting wounds.

We'd both fit into that velvet chair nicely, Oliver and me, studying every night by candlelight or kerosene lamp, hip to hip, a mass of overlapping legs. Our hands all over each other in the shadows. Susan's fat rear didn't fit so well, I guess; she parked it in a wicker chair next to Oliver's throne. Every few minutes she'd lean over and shove her tongue down his throat.

That night—yes, I mean Sunday the 3rd—was far from the first time I'd been faced with that disgusting sight of course. But by nightfall I was so restless I couldn't stay trapped in my room any longer. Static packed the air in that styrofoamy way it does before a lightning storm, when it hasn't rained for weeks. I ran out into the road to stare at the flaming orange sunset. It bore down on my head, oppressive, squashing my skull until I couldn't stand the pressure. I wanted the sky to split down the middle like a pair of tight silk pants on a fat rump. Something has to change, I was thinking as I headed into the cornfield for my usual walk along the mowed paths that stripe the farmers' fields.

Yes, I know about the rumors. How could Oliver say such terrible things about me? I don't understand, when our bodies once twined so softly together, like flowering bindweeds and made us one. I guess Daddy tried to warn me. "No girl of mine is going off to study evil at some fancy mixed-sex college!" He'd told me when I said I was getting myself an education. "I won't see you in some uni-institution, to unlearn you all my work! A Christian must keep apart from the World, Rebekah."

I wasn't listening too well. Maybe he was right after all. I don't miss Daddy, though. I never liked the wild way he looked at me after Momma went in the ground. I won myself this scholarship and I meant to use it. Well, wouldn't you?

44

"I admonish you," Daddy lectured me, "if you do not serve Jehovah, Rebekah, then you serve evil and must be cast out. Don't forget who is invisible ruler of the world. You commit the sin of omission, omitting your sacred duty to Jehovah and your family. For that, you won't be among the 144,000, and you have no place in my house!"

"It's not much of a house anyway!" I said, slamming the back door in such a way it came off the top hinges like it often did. That was the last I saw of him. I made my way over to the Trailways station with my bags. Never looked back. When the college housing lady assigned me this off-campus farmhouse-looking place nestled by the cornfield, with its rickety stairs, peeling green shutters, eye-popping sugar maples—I was in bliss. The place was enough like home to let me remember Momma, but full of laughing people my own age to help me forget Daddy.

Oliver's room was right across the hall from the kitchen and when the semester started, he'd come out in the mornings and we'd have breakfast together on the sun porch before class. A few weeks later, when autumn frosted the grass, we started going into his room instead, our bodies slapping together like choppy waves on a winter lake.

We talked about everything under the sun. When he looked in my eyes so serious and said he understood, I felt reborn. I was only thinking aloud, but I told him I wasn't sure about religion anymore, if it really made people's better, or only fogged up their minds.

I knew I was in sin, in great sin, and Daddy would be here with his gun in a flash if he ever knew. But I'd given up on Daddy. That gun came out whenever anybody came near his property or used some word he didn't like. Everyone in our old town said he was nuttier than peanut butter. I wondered myself if we did the right thing, not getting Momma the transfusions. The doctor was furious—he said, "Ferris, you might as well shoot her

45

yourself!" Daddy was adamant, wouldn't listen to me either. I owed him nothing. Maybe I had a duty to Jehovah, but what about my duty to myself? If He loved me as I hoped He did, He wouldn't want me to pass up my chance for happiness with Oliver who said he loved me. He was the light I'd waited for so long.

All winter I was dying for spring to come and invite us back onto the sun porch. Sometimes I'd return from class to find Oliver at the kitchen table deep in conversation with one of our housemates, Rick or Jill or Susan. One day I opened the front door to the sound of Susan's squeals echoing down the hall from Oliver's room. I never said a word, heaven knows. Momma always told me God looks after us better than we can guard ourselves. I took a leap of faith and decided I'd leave my woes to Him, praying only for the day Oliver would see how great love our love was, and return to my arms. Patience is a virtue. I knew he'd only recognize what we'd had together if I let him come around on his own. Yes, of course it was hard living in the same house with those two lovers. But you see, I knew their union was only a pale version of our eternal bond.

When summer came near, I couldn't pray anymore. I knew Oliver was unworthy of me, playing his teasing games in view of my window to torture me, but I still pined for him. I'd sketch or paint with watercolors late in the night—yes, including these drawings you keep going on about, of the two of them consumed by hell-flames. I only painted what I saw in my mind's eye! Oliver and Susan weren't the kind who cared about love, only selfish pleasure. I could imagine them so clearly, burning down there in hell, their wicked tongues forking together as their bodies glowed red hot and crumbled to ash.

While everyone else in our dorm house was in class, I tried to reclaim the empty sun porch, only to find their two presences filling up the chairs like life-sized inflatable dolls. The wind blew so hot through the screens it drove me out. Even the house didn't want me. I tried going to class or reading in the library, but it was no good at all, my mind was never where I was. At sunset I'd leave on my walks, coming in after dark when it was cooler and the lovers were behind locked doors. No, it wasn't unusual for me to walk outside late, if that's what you're asking. My other housemates can tell you—they're all okay, aren't they? Good. I thought so. Please don't look at me that way!

That Sunday night, yes, the 3rd, I kept my eye on that lobster sunset so I could slip past the sun porch without seeing their ugly faces mashed together. I was thinking Daddy might be crazy, but I'd been caught up in worldly passion. I'd neglected my duty; why else would He punish me so, to make my days living hell? I was cast out. I'd ruined my scholarship, missed so many classes I saw no point in studying for finals. When school ended, I would have noplace to go.

I cut through the cornfield on a muddy side path. A few days before that, I'd seen a young farmer's son coming the other way, and I'd let my dress slip off my shoulders and pulled him down in the field with me. I thought maybe we'd cross paths again. No, I don't know his name. No one was around. Alone in the corn, I stopped and held my breath, listening to the stalks thrusting their young shoots up through the papery older leaves. I'd hoped the sound of thriving life would bring me some peace, but it only reminded me of the rustling in Oliver's bedroom the other night when I put my ear to the door, the humping of silk underclothes barely softening the sharp moans.

Heat lightning at the edges of the sky twitched a nerve. My faith was flickering. I lifted my arms to the sky and surrendered my sorry soul. If there was a Jehovah, maybe

He was not on my team. Or, if I'd done so many wrongs I deserved to suffer, I begged a thunderbolt would strike me. Maybe a water moccasin slithering from the irrigation ditch to bite my ankle. If no messenger of death came, maybe what the philosophy professor said was true— that He didn't exist in any literal form. If so, even my soul had nowhere to go. I hoped that wasn't my fate.

To give Him a little more time to declare Himself just in case, I threw myself on the ground by the irrigation ditch, shiny in the moonlight like a poisonous mercury river and cried my heart out, waiting for the pinch of fangs. There was no thunderbolt or serpent. A wind came up and thrashed the half-grown cornstalks. Voices in the corn began to hiss and chuckle: *hhsss sssSatan lovesss you,* I thought they said. I didn't want to go back to the dorm, but I was shivering, I was so afraid of those voices. I said a last prayer: "Give me reason to hope." Then I got up and ran in the dark until I stumbled onto the road not far from the house.

Light leaked from the sun porch through the pores of the screens. I could see it from the road, and I wanted to scream! Well, because *I* wanted to sit out there. But Oliver and Susan hadn't gone upstairs yet. I didn't know what I would say to them, but I charged across the lawn toward the sun porch instead of heading to the front door. Forces stirred around me in the dry wind. They seemed to propel me. Elemental forces, you know? I felt sparks in my fingertips as my feet scuffed the grass.

The light inside the sun porch leaped like it was alive. I stood up on tiptoe and squinted through the screen. Susan and Oliver were asleep in their chairs, side-by-side. A candle flame flickered and throbbed, stretched up to a tall, thin exclamation point. Oliver always loved to burn candles, propping them in the mouth of a Chianti bottle. The wick was upright, but the taper had slipped sideways a bit. Oliver was snoring, sitting up straight with his mouth hanging open. I was shocked to see a bottle full of brandy and two glasses on the crate-table. Oliver had never touched liquor in my presence.

Susan! She must have corrupted him. Her hand dangled off Oliver's big bony knee, and she'd half-fallen against him in her drunken sleep. Her face was pasty in the candlelight, dark eye make-up gluey on her eyelids. I noticed a carelessly wadded-up **Times** someone had flung on top of the crate table. A big gust of wind fluttered Susan's bangs and flapped the pages of Oliver's spiral notebook loudly, but they didn't wake up. I couldn't see inside the porch very well, so I'm not sure exactly how it started. No, I never went inside. I did *not* touch the screen door onto the porch; you can dust it for fingerprints if you want! All I know is, a bright light flowed out around me like gold ink and soaked into Oliver's notebook. It spread in such a gentle motion like a cat licking her fur, yet so blinding I didn't grasp what I was seeing at first. Then the crate was a block of orange neon. I guess the candle must have blown over in that last gust.

I don't know how long! I lost track. It seemed in-stantaneous. I felt this terrible heat in my face and my eyes watered. I wanted to back away but before I could move, a ring of fire sprouted up around the sides of the porch. It *did* look a bit like my watercolors, this one here especially where the fire's all around them, but I painted those weeks ago. *You* know I haven't been back to my room since then—they won't let me!

Oliver and Susan didn't wake up, no. I couldn't make a sound. How would you feel? My mind was racing. They must have been quite drunk. Of course I knew I had to get help! All human laws that don't conflict with God's laws must be obeyed, I know that. My three other housemates were asleep upstairs, and every single thing I owned was inside. I was afraid to go in to use the phone. That would've been stupid, with flames near the door. I ran down the road toward campus, figuring I'd find a phone and call 911. I looked for doors to knock on, but it must've been very late—I have no idea what time. The windows of the neighbor's houses were blank except one giving off a blue TV glow. I ran on the porch, wondering how the people inside could be wrapped up some canned TV drama. Just as I was about to knock, I heard two loud pops in the distance, two wet explosions one right after the other. Seconds later, rain came splattering down like someone had turned on a faucet. I was soaked immediately. No fire could last long in that kind of downpour. Then I knew for sure what it all meant, what this night was a sign of.

Pretty soon, the sirens came: one, two, three fire trucks roaring up the street. I guess between them and the rain, the house was pretty much spared, right? I'll bet the porch was the only badly burnt part, and that's how you found the drawings in my room. You can keep them. I don't care, but can I have my other things back now, since you won't let me go get them? Please, it's all I own. I haven't done anything wrong.

What do you mean, how do I sleep at night? I sleep great, of course! Especially now that I know I don't have to fear evil anymore. With my own eyes I've seen solid proof. I know that the wicked will indeed be eternally destroyed just as it's written, for Jehovah protects the good and the innocent, and answers our prayers.

Encanto

All week, the women at the silicon chip plant where I'm Day Manager have been stuffing my ears with tall tales. All this bruja-ha is their way of telling me it's no secret anymore that Annamaria and I are lovers.

"Before you know it, Mr. Layton," Mercedes whispers, "the honeysuckle vines outside your bedroom window will creep in and wrap around your neck." She pauses outside the clean room to snap her latex glove, a sinister, bonecrack of a sound. Playfully, she winks as her ghostly thin form, plastic-garbed to keep out the dust of death, slithers through the triple doors into the sanctum like smoke.

"Yez," agrees the crone in her European accent, thick as French fish sauce: "You nice man, but short in living. There is lot you not know of zis world."

I smile gamely as one by one they don their Saran shrouds. "Mark my word," Jalou hisses, last to go in. Her gaze fixes on the most distant point in the room—its hangar-like doors. "You'll wake from a bad dream feeling like an iron plate sits on your chest, crushing the air out, and you'll decide it doesn't matter, you no longer care about anything. It happened to the one before you. It happens to all of them when she is through. Should I tell you their names, Tom Layton?"

"No thanks, Jalou" I humor her. These women and their jealous games! How do they know so much? They must be spying on my love and me! Mari, as I call her, works the night shift, so these woman never see her. I would never have seen her sweet face myself if Claire and I hadn't fought that night. I picture these women whispering to each other, *"Why does Annamaria get to ride in the manager's shiny beemer car? Is she better than us?"* But at least they spin their silly yarns with a wink and a snap of humor.

This afternoon it's no longer a joke. Mari, I've just heard, was fired from the company. I'm so enraged, I take lunch in my office instead of mingling with the workers in the cafeteria as usual. No one hinted this was coming.

I confront Jesch in his office. He's the boss; you know it from the way he looms behind his desk, though he isn't a large man. He stands up as I come in, leaning forward on his palms like a human tripod. The dark-framed glasses on his square politician's face perch at the tip of his pale, flabby nose. They seem to have absorbed his whole personality. "Tom, I must ask you to sit down," he says.

Only after I've taken my seat will he settle back into the plush leather lap of his chair and speak. I have to command my fists to unclench at my sides.

"Why?" Jesch voices the question for me. *"Why* did I let her go? Ask Mercedes Alcala. Ask Trina, or Rafaela. " His plump hands flop outward on the desk, palms upward, a fleshy open book.

I remind him what rumors are: mythical chimeras that take on lives of their own.

Jesch continues dismissively, "Tom. The fact that she lives in your house is enough to convince anyone you're bewitched. You can't get rid of her."

I leap to my feet. "I have no desire to get rid of her!"

"You think you don't." He shakes his head with vigor. "That's just it."

"What has she ever done to anyone? Give it to me straight."

Jesch looks away, a sigh hissing through his teeth, and doesn't answer. He's probably thinking of my wife Claire, in the hospital. Poor Claire. My decision must seem abrupt to her, but the fact is, we don't belong together. It's absurd what they say, that Mari caused Claire's pneumonia. As Mari said to me once: "It takes two to make an adultery. The adulterer, and the one who waits for love to take its course instead of loving." I take my seat again, quietly.

"It's over between me and Claire," I remind Jesch, tenting my hands over my crossed knees in a rational manner. "We've always had difficulties."

"Claire deserves better, Tom. Bottom line: As long as that woman stays at your house, we've got a problem. She makes us all extremely nervous."

"Why?"

Jesch gets up and minces around his desk but doesn't answer.

"Are you threatening me, Sir? That might not be wise," I caution. Jesch likes his profit margins high, high enough to staff the facility with dozens of illegal residents whisked back and forth over the Tijuana border in his own private bus. He pays these special commuters a quarter of what legal staff earn.

"I've made no threats!" Jesch's face is the picture of puzzled innocence. "You violated our policy by dating an employee."

"She's not—"

"I'll give you until next Friday to think it over. That's eight days. We'll discuss this again at that time. I believe you'll see things more clearly then." He turns to face the window, confident I'll be gone when next he turns around.

He's giving me the old tomato! How does he mean to keep me in check, should I decide to report his seamy activities? His confidence is eerie, chilling. Leaving his office in a blind rage, I bump the doorframe with my shoulder and don't feel the pain until hours later.

In bed Mari sees the bruise and cups her hand over it. I'm lying on my back half-asleep. The cool touch on my sore, hot flesh makes me sit up suddenly. Her eyes are bright and close to mine, startling as flame. Then her lips curve upward so sweetly, my anxiety fades. I reach up to hold her small chin, admiring her, my orchid. She needs no special reason to smile, the way children do.

By morning, the bruise has nearly vanished. The only pain I feel is the sting of leaving Mari for the day. Now there is only a week left to decide if I have finally found the love of my life, in which case no sacrifice, job or Claire is too great. Or am I a middleaged fool under a spell, about to lose everything?

When I come in to work Monday, Holly the receptionist pouts, "You aren't yourself these days, Tom." Holly and I once had an amiable, flirtatious friendship, but I tired of her bronco-queen style. "What potion is she feeding you?"

"Look." I level a forefinger at Holly's two-inch false eyelashes. "This is the 21st century, so can we drop the witchhunt? I'm fucking sick of it!"

"Temper, temper!" Holly's head jerks back from my imaginary slap-in-the-face. "Come on, Tom. Annamaria's descended from one of those ancient tribes. They have dark secrets, peyote rituals. Didn't you read those Castaneda books?"

"Racist bitch," I say under my breath, waving pleasantly to Jesch at the far end of the corridor.

"Honey, you never used to sweet-talk me like that," Holly drones in my ear.

I turn in disgust.

Holly hisses after me, "Tom, they say she saw her whole family slaughtered in Medellin. That she blamed the Americans. She lives only for vengeance. Mercedes should know; they're cousins. That woman made her lose two babies."

I come home with a fierce headache that night, a steady throbbing behind the eyes so intense my vision twinkles. Mari stands behind my chair, rubbing salve into my temples. I stare at the mural she's been painting, her project since she left the job. A raw canvas is stretched the length of the dining room wall, and on it, a tempest of colors, startling, bright, intricate shapes twined together: vines, animals, waves, turrets, trees. Each time I come home it has grown, taken on new colors and dimensions. Mari calls it "the Garden of Our Love" and from here, it does resemble a lush tropical paradise where I'd dwell happily forever if she's with me.

But the rumors burn inside me. "Guess what Highhorse Holly said today?" In my most ironic tone, I repeat Holly's slurs about tribal sorcery.

I hear laughter behind me, trickles of sparks like kisses down my spine. Mari leans on my shoulder, smiling against my cheek. "We are all, everyone, descended from ancient tribes, Tom. Even Holly." Mari's hair cascades down my bare chest, a bolt of earth-black silk unfolding. "Everyone has spells to cast, but they have limited magic, power that charms only certain people. If that person stops needing what the spell offers, it breaks. But who is this Castaneda? Is he like Casanova?"

"No, my love." I'm caught up in her amusement. Then I notice the salve she's been using on my temples; it's the color of fresh blood. The tiny jar she scoops it from has no label. I feel a little jolt of cold nerves. "What makes the ointment that color, Mari?" I ask.

"Cochineal," she says calmly. "A kind of beetles."

"Uhg," I make a face. "Sexy."

"Mmm, yes." She covers my oiled temples with kisses to demonstrate how safe the ointment is. "See? Non-toxic, like crayola." She glances at her art table.

I toss out a non sequitur, "Holly says Mercedes has lost many children."

"My poor cousin," Mari sighs, confirming her relationship to Mercedes, just as Holly said. "Mercedes had many abortions when she was young. Maybe it hurt her womb. It's sad, now that she wants a child." Mari gazes into my eyes and asks if I am feeling better now. I lift my head. The pain is gone. Yes, I smile. With her I can't help it, smiles just come. Before I know it we're making love again and I feel such joy. Nothing ever before in my life has approached it.

But is it true what happened in Columbia? That, I can't ask.

By the bathroom sink is another unmarked jar of crushed leaves erupting with the minty smell I know as Pennyroyal, which I've read can empty the womb.

Four days left to decide—a world asunder. Claire phones my office from the hospital, begging me to visit. Her pneumonia's worse, she claims; they've put her back on oxygen. I don't believe her. Her chest sounds clearer than it did last we spoke. More likely, Claire thinks a visit will change my mind, that if I come and see her in her plight, pity will flood me and love will float on its tide. But that won't happen since it was never love. "The house is yours when you're well," I promise, and hang up quickly. She mustn't hear the tremors in my voice. She'll take them for something else.

I leave work early, afraid she'll call back. I know Claire won't dare call the house. Since Mari was fired from the plant, she's been answering my telephone.

Wednesday I feel rested and peaceful at work, secure in my decision, impervious to Holly's sidelong glances. I stop at a travel agency on the way home and pick up piles of colorful pamphlets—Bermuda, Majorca, St. Moritz. I always wanted to take off on a whim and go far away, but Claire would insist on three or four weeks simply to plan the itinerary, three more to pack, and I didn't see the point.

When I walk into the house, laughing like a madman, I greet Mari with my avalanche of glossy dream voyages. "Which country would you like to see? Pick one, and we'll go."

"Really?" She breaks into her slow smile and reaches for my hand.

I let her pull me inside. "We can't very well stay here, can we?"

Her arms are around me even as the door closes. "Tom. You mean live far away? Is that the best thing for you? Your job, the work you love! I can't ruin—"

"You couldn't ruin anything! I know what I'm doing."

The smile evaporates even from her eyes. "You must think carefully what's best for you. Don't concern with me. I always get by. Nothing ruins *me*."

I clutch her, alarmed by this talk, the way her eyes have stopped seeing. Her glowing brown skin's gone ashy. "Believe me, *you're* what's best for me!"

"Come, look. Our Garden of Love is almost finished," she says leading me over to her mural. When I stare closely into the rich, fantastical topography, I find numerous tiny, tender objects worked into the details, shapes I never noticed from a distance: hearts, a peacock, a koala, miniature palm trees, a dime-sized palace.

"It looks like Eden," I say. "You're so talented!"

"No. It's just what I see," she protests, frowning deeply as if I've insulted her.

Today's Thursday. I've decided to wait until the very last moment, Friday morning, to tell Jesch I'm leaving. I've been careful not to drop the slightest hint. In fact no one asks, no one so much as speaks to me. Lately, my co-workers treat me like a villain, answering my questions in grunts, hardly nodding when I greet them. All for the sake of a few rumors, a pang of jealousy, seasoned with lies. An amusing soap opera for the exquisitely bored.

Mari explains it to me: "They think only of power, like politicians do. Nobody likes a person who has power and doesn't use it as *they* would. They'd rather see that power destroyed than let someone else hold it in their hands."

What power does she speak of? She's an extraordinary beauty, the envy of other women, but is that all? Sometimes I fear that she's stumbled on some secret Jesch can't allow out of the bag, something she saw or overheard during the night shift, and that's why he fired her. Perhaps she's a danger to him, and thus to me. I don't always understand Mari's reasoning, but I believe that time will quell these doubts. Each night we spend together, I come closer to giving up my fears, closer to accepting who she is, regardless of what that may be.

Thursday night when I get home, Mari's out, probably at the corner bodega. I wait impatiently on the couch for the peace her presence will bring, reading my newspapers, then pacing the living room like an addict expecting a promised, and overdue, fix. As the sky darkens and the city lights come up around me, my heart begins to pound sickeningly. I stare at Mari's mural until the moment I know I must take a look around the house.

Her things, yes, they're gone: her jeans, her walking shoes, her vials of salves and powders. I know even before I begin to search that there's no note. Still, I turn the place upside down, clearing tabletops with a swipe of my arm, dumping drawers, panting for clues until I'm exhausted, crying for a scrap of evidence, anything. Finally I stand breathless in front of the finished mural, which now occupies every centimeter of the wall, all the sketching colored in. The lighting is dim; I bring in a sunlamp, and the cat, and we inspect it together.

She has done this for me. Because rumors are so powerful and I'm so weak, she has fled. It's proof of her love—I'm sure of that. For she knew it wasn't until tomorrow that I'd make my final move with Jesch. Unless, of course, the move was his.

Again I examine the mural, every dazzling, fluorescent inch of it, but I was right the first time: there are no human figures in it. There is no one in the garden.